There was much to celebrate at Pride Rock. The evil Scar was gone. The Pride Lands were at peace. The spirit of good King Mufasa looked down upon the happy kingdom as old Rafiki, the baboon, presented the newborn cub of King Simba and Queen Nala to the cheering animals below.

Pumbaa and Timon were excited about the fun they were going to have with the new cub. "I'm telling you, buddy, it's gonna be like old times. You, me, and the little guy…"

But old Rafiki knew they were not quite correct. "It is a girl!"

Pumbaa and Timon looked over at cute little Kiara. "Girl?" They both fainted!

As Kiara grew older, she wanted to explore the Pride Lands. But Simba always warned her, "And stay away from the Outlands."

Kiara jumped into the tall grass. She ran farther and farther away from Pride Rock, and soon she came to a swampy river with a fallen tree. Crossing the river, Kiara met another lion cub. The two cubs hopped from log to log, staring at each other. "Who are you, Pride Lander?"

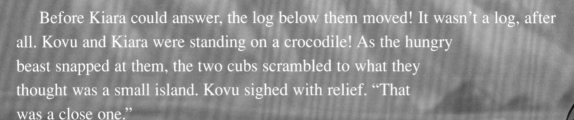

Before Kiara could answer, the log below them moved! It wasn't a log, after all. Kovu and Kiara were standing on a crocodile! As the hungry beast snapped at them, the two cubs scrambled to what they thought was a small island. Kovu sighed with relief. "That was a close one."

"Yeah!"

But this island moved too! It was a group of crocodiles! Kiara jumped to safety in a tree. Kovu leapt from croc to croc—until he ran out of crocs! Then, just as a huge reptile was about to sink its sharp teeth into Kovu, Kiara jumped on its head, shutting its powerful jaws. "I did it! I did it!"

Kiara was very excited. "He just totally ate me up right there, and I jumped on his head and I bopped him so good! We make such a good team! And you…you were really brave."

"Yeah? You were pretty brave too. My name's Kovu."

"I'm Kiara. Tag. You're it!"

The two cubs laughed and played. But nearby, Zira was listening and snarling. She leapt in front of Kovu.

At the same time, Simba seemed to spring out of nowhere to protect Kiara. He faced the snarling lioness. "I banished you from the Pride Lands. Now you and your young cub, get out!"

"These lands belong to Scar."

"Take him and get out. We're finished here."

"Oh no, Simba. We have barely begun." Zira grabbed Kovu and slinked away.

Simba was upset that Kiara had disobeyed him. "One day I won't be here, and I need you to carry on in my place. You are part of the great circle of—"

"—circle of life. I know." Kiara had heard these words many times before.

"Exactly, and you need to be careful. As future queen—"

"What if I don't want to be queen? It's no fun."

"That's like saying you don't want to be a lion. It's in your blood, as I am. We are part of each other. As long as you live here, it's who you are. You'll understand someday."

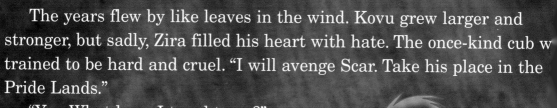

The years flew by like leaves in the wind. Kovu grew larger and stronger, but sadly, Zira filled his heart with hate. The once-kind cub w trained to be hard and cruel. "I will avenge Scar. Take his place in the Pride Lands."

"Yes. What have I taught you?"

"Simba is the enemy."

"And what must you do?"

"I must kill him!"

They planned to have Kovu befriend Kiara, so he could sneak up on Simba.

Over the years, Kiara had also grown up. It was time for the brave young lioness to go off on her first hunt. Simba asked Timon and Pumbaa to follow and make sure she was safe.

Kiara tried to stalk a herd of antelope, but she made too much noise. The herd scampered off.

Zira's cubs, Nuka and Vitani, watched from a distance. The two lions were eager to carry out Zira's evil plan. Nuka waved a flaming branch as they both ran down a hill. He lit a patch of dry grass.

"Roasty toasty princess . . . roasty toasty princess!"

High on a hill, Zira smiled as she and Kovu watched the grass burst into flame.

"The plan is in motion. Go!"

Kovu dashed into the fire.

Deadly smoke choked Kiara. But just before she fainted, Kovu picked her up and carried her to safety.

When Simba learned what Kovu had done, he was suspicious. "You saved her? Why?"

"I humbly ask to join your pride."

Simba was unsure. "For now I reserve judgment. We'll see who you really are."

Kiara was grateful to Kovu for saving her life. Kovu offered to teach her how to be a better hunter. "All right. Impress me. We start at dawn."

The sun was peeking over the Pride Lands as Kovu took Kiara for her hunting lesson.

"Shhh. Watch the master. And learn." Kovu was about to pounce on his prey when Kiara heard a familiar voice.

"Aaaah! Don't eat me. Please!"

"Timon! What are you doing here?"

"This just happens to be the best smorgasbord in the Pride Lands. Bugs everywhere." But poor Timon, a flock of birds swooped down over his breakfast. "Go on! Shoo! Shoo!"

Pumbaa looked at Kovu and had an idea. "Hey, maybe he could help."

Kovu roared a mighty roar, and the birds flew away. Timon, Pumbaa, and Kiara chased them, but Kovu was confused. "Why are we doing this? What's the point of this training?"

"Training? This is just for fun."

Across the Pride Lands, the crazy group charged after the birds. Even Kovu was enjoying himself.

"Yeehaw!"

The clever birds flew
into a canyon. When Kiara,
Kovu, Timon, and Pumbaa
followed, they found
themselves face to
face with a crash of rhino.
It wasn't long before the four
of them ran out with the
whole crash at their heels.
They squeezed into a crevice
in a large boulder just as the
rhinos thundered past the
little group.

Safe within the tiny nook, Kiara, Timon, Pumbaa, and Kovu laughed with relief. Kovu couldn't believe how much fun he was having. "What a blast!"

Timon gave Kovu a friendly hug. "You're okay, kid."

He and Pumbaa began to wiggle out of the tight space. "Excuse me. Pardon me. Pardon me. That's it. That's it.  That's it." But as they did so, Kiara and Kovu were pushed close together. Close enough to kiss. Kiara blushed as she and Kovu squeezed out of the crevice.

The next morning, Kovu practiced telling Kiara the truth. "Kiara, Zira had a plot, and I was part of it, but I don't want to be. It's because I love you."

But before Kovu could talk to Kiara, Simba invited him for a walk. Simba explained the truth about Scar. "Scar couldn't let go of his hate, and in the end, it destroyed him."

Kovu understood. "He truly was a killer."

Simba looked around the burnt forest. "Fire is a killer." He found a tiny green sprout growing among the ashes. "Sometimes what's left behind can grow better than the generation before, if given the chance."

All of a sudden, Simba was surrounded by a vicious band of lionesses, led by Zira. "Well done, Kovu. Just like we always planned."

Kovu tried to stop the attack. "No! I didn't have anything to do with this!"

But it was too late. Sharp teeth and claws lunged at Simba from all directions. Simba's only escape was up the face of a cliff.

Zira screamed to her son. "Get him, Kovu! Get him! Do it now!" But Kovu didn't respond.

Simba made it up the cliff, and just in time. Kovu ran to Zira's side. "I didn't mean to. It wasn't my fault. I did nothing."

"Exactly. And in doing so, you betrayed your pride, betrayed Scar."

"I want nothing more to do with him."

"You cannot escape it. Nuka is dead because of you. You've killed your own brother."

"No!"

Kovu returned to the Pride Lands, but Simba would not forgive him. "When you first came here, you asked for judgment. And I pass it now. EXILE!"

Kovu left the Pride Lands in disgrace, but Kiara still believed in him. "Father, please! Reconsider. You don't know him."

"I know he's following in Scar's paw prints. And I must follow in my father's."

"You will never be Mufasa!" Kiara ran from her father in tears.

That rainy night, Simba's friend Zazu braved the storm to deliver an urgent message. "Sire, the Outsiders are on the attack. It's war!"

Simba's pride soon faced Zira's warriors at each end of Antelope Gorge. This was the moment Zira had been waiting for. "It's over, Simba! I have dreamed of nothing else for years. Attack!"

A terrible battle, lit only by lightning, began to rage in the pounding rain.

Zira saw her chance to attack Simba herself. "Simba. You're mine."

The other lions watched as Zira and Simba fought bitterly. Then out of the darkness came Kovu and Kiara. "Daddy, this has to stop!"

Zira growled at her son. "Get out of the way."

"You'll never hurt Kiara or Simba. Not while I'm here."

Kiara crept closer to her father. "A wise king once told me, we are one. I didn't understand him then. Now I do."

"Let it go, Zira. It's time to put the past behind us."

"I'll never let it go!" Zira leapt at Simba, but Kiara jumped in her way. The two lionesses went tumbling down Antelope Gorge, just as the log jam at the mouth of the gorge gave way to the rushing river.

Zira dangled over the edge of a rock. Kiara reached out her paw. "Zira, come on. I'll help you!"

But Zira slipped away and was lost forever in the churning rapids.

After the battle had past, everyone gathered at Pride Rock. Simba and Nala, Kiara and Kovu, all the former Outsiders, and the rest of Simba's pride completed the circle of friendship.

Nearby, Timon, Pumbaa, and Zazu watched the ceremony. Pumbaa cried. "I love moments like this!"

The mighty lions roared as hundreds of other animals shared their joy.

Above it all, Mufasa looked down upon them, especially at his beloved Simba. "Well done, my son. We are one!"